This book belongs to

Ms. Jarvis

For my niece, Marianna Elise Tarpley,
the loveliest princess of them all:
may you always live in the knowledge
of your greatness. And may all
your dreams come true. —N.A.T.

To Bianca and Tayler Buck—J.F.

Printed in the United States of America

The movie *The Princess and the Frog* Copyright © 2009 Disney, story inspired in part by the book
The Frog Princess by E.D. Baker Copyright © 2002, published by Bloomsbury Publishing, Inc.

First Edition   10 9 8 7 6 5 4 3 2 1

Library of Congress Cataloging-in-Publication data on file.

ISBN 978-1-4231-1859-6

Visit www.disneybooks.com

PRINCESS TIANA
and the
Royal Ball

By Natasha Anastasia Tarpley

Illustrated by James Finch

Disney PRESS

New York

A crowd of hungry people was lined up at Tiana's Palace, waiting for their chance to sample the restaurant's famous beignets. It was rumored throughout all of New Orleans that the pastries were magical. They made *dreams come true.* . . .

After all, look at what happened to Tiana.

She'd become a *frog,*

fallen in *love,*

married a frog *prince . . .* and become a real *princess.*

To top it all off, she now owned the *restaurant of her dreams!*

As Princess Tiana looked out over the elegant
dining room, Sam, the restaurant's maître d', handed her
an envelope. "This just arrived, madame."
A moment later, Princess Tiana heard a familiar voice.

"*Yoo-hoo, Tia!*" It was Charlotte, Princess Tiana's best friend. "I was just out doing a little shopping and thought I'd say a quick how-do."

Tiana rushed to greet her friend.

"Wait!" Charlotte held up her hand. "I must greet you proper-like. I know *royal protocol.* Princess Tiana." She curtsied, sweeping her arm elaborately.

"Oh, Lottie, stop it!" Tiana giggled and pulled Charlotte into a big bear hug.

Charlotte's eyes fell on the envelope that Princess Tiana had just received.

She *plucked* it out of her friend's hand.

She lifted the envelope to her ear and *shook* it.

Then she *ran her fingers* along the elegant lettering and carefully inspected the gold seal.

"If this is what I think it is, you are about to have the thrill of your life!" Charlotte said excitedly.

Tiana rolled her eyes and began to open the envelope *ever-so-slowly.*

Charlotte waited and waited. *"Open it!"* she shrieked when she couldn't stand the suspense any longer.

Tiana pulled out a fancy invitation. "Naveen's mother and father are in town. They're inviting Naveen and me to a royal ball tonight."

"I knew it!" Charlotte exploded. "Oh, Tia, do you know what this means? *Do you,*

do you,

DO YOU?"

"It's only your *first ball*—to show the world that you are a real live princess!" Charlotte explained.

Tiana sighed. "I know I'm a princess. I don't have to prove it to the world."

"Of course *I* know that you're a princess, *cherie*. But this is your moment to shine as *Princess* Tiana."

Charlotte whipped a thick book from her purse. "Good thing I always carry this," she said.

"We've got so much work to do:

we have to find you a dress,

pick out shoes,

style your hair . . ."

"How 'bout we start with lunch?
Princesses do need to eat,"
Tiana said.

In just a few moments, the waiter came by.

Charlotte wagged her finger. "You're not really going to eat *that*, are you?"

"Why not?" Tiana frowned. "This is my daddy's famous gumbo."

"As a princess you must eat only the best and fanciest cuisine. See, it says right here. . . ." Charlotte pointed to a page in the handbook.

Tiana *sighed*. Maybe she ought to give Charlotte's rules a chance.

After all, Lottie had been studying this princess
stuff her whole life. . . .

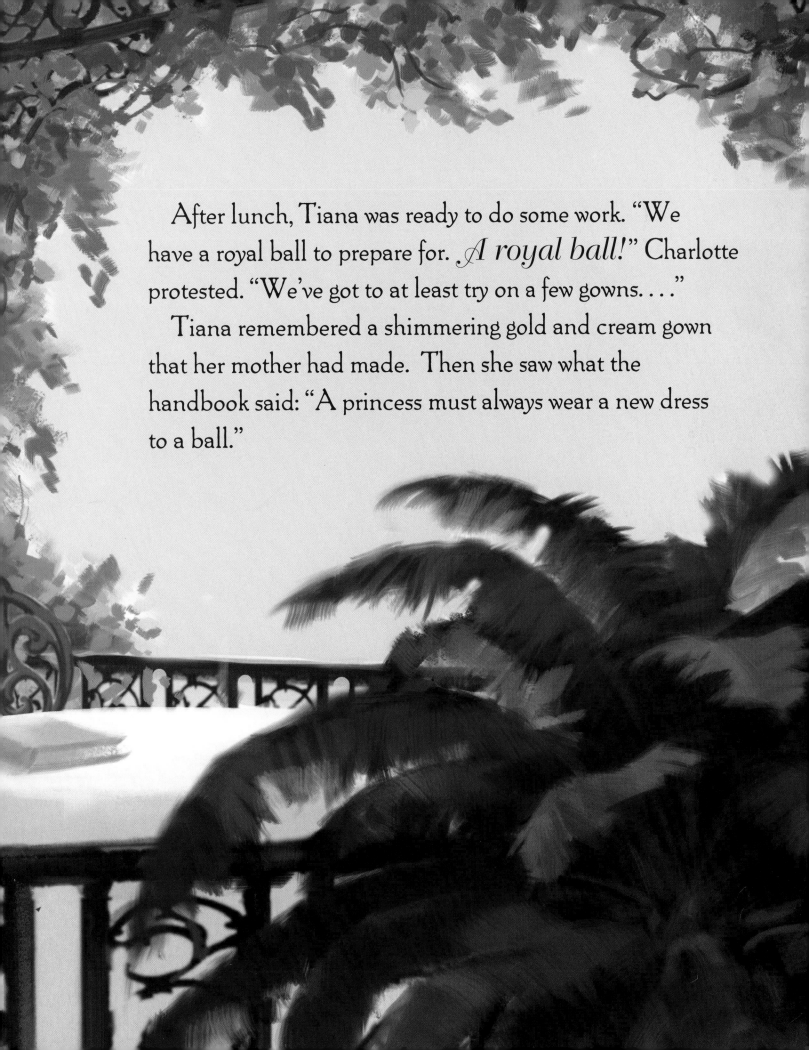

After lunch, Tiana was ready to do some work. "We have a royal ball to prepare for. *A royal ball!*" Charlotte protested. "We've got to at least try on a few gowns...."

Tiana remembered a shimmering gold and cream gown that her mother had made. Then she saw what the handbook said: "A princess must always wear a new dress to a ball."

"But there's no way Mama can make one in time," Tiana protested.

Before long, Charlotte had taken her friend to the *finest* dress shop in New Orleans.

Tiana tried on one dress.

Then another . . .

. . . and another.

"Lottie, you've dressed me up like a *peppermint stick,* a *pineapple,* and a *pumpkin,*" Tiana said. "Seems like I'm shopping for dinner instead of a ball."

"I'll have you know that these are the latest designs from *Par-ee.* That's how they say Paris, by the way." Charlotte crossed her arms. "'A princess must be aware of the latest fashion trends.'"

Just then, Sam burst into the shop, which was just across the street from the restaurant. "Sorry, Princess, but we have an emergency. Chef Henri *changed* the beignet recipe, and the customers are sending them back!"

The princess set the ball gowns aside and left.
"Just a second, let's see what the handbook has to say about this . . ." Charlotte called, trailing after Tiana.

"Chef Henri! What's this about you changing the beignets?"

"They are so, how do you say . . . *plain*, no?" the chef replied. "I wanted to make them a little fancier."

Tiana remembered how her daddy used the simplest ingredients to stir up a pot of something wonderful. "Fancy doesn't always mean better," she said.

"You are right, madame," Chef Henri agreed. "Please forgive me."

Tiana smiled.

"But, but, he changed your recipe! A princess would *never* forgive such behavior!" Charlotte blurted out. "The handbook says—"

"Lottie, I've had enough of your old handbook!" Tiana said. "A *real princess* understands that everyone makes mistakes sometimes."

As she spoke, Tiana realized that she didn't need a bunch of silly rules to tell her how to be a princess. All she needed to do was follow her own heart.

"I'm sorry, Tia. I was just trying to help," Charlotte apologized.

"I know you meant well, cherie," Tiana said. She grinned mischievously. "Now, do you really want to help?"

Charlotte nodded.

"Will you accompany Prince Naveen and me to the ball tonight?"

"*Oh, yes!*" Charlotte clapped her hands together.

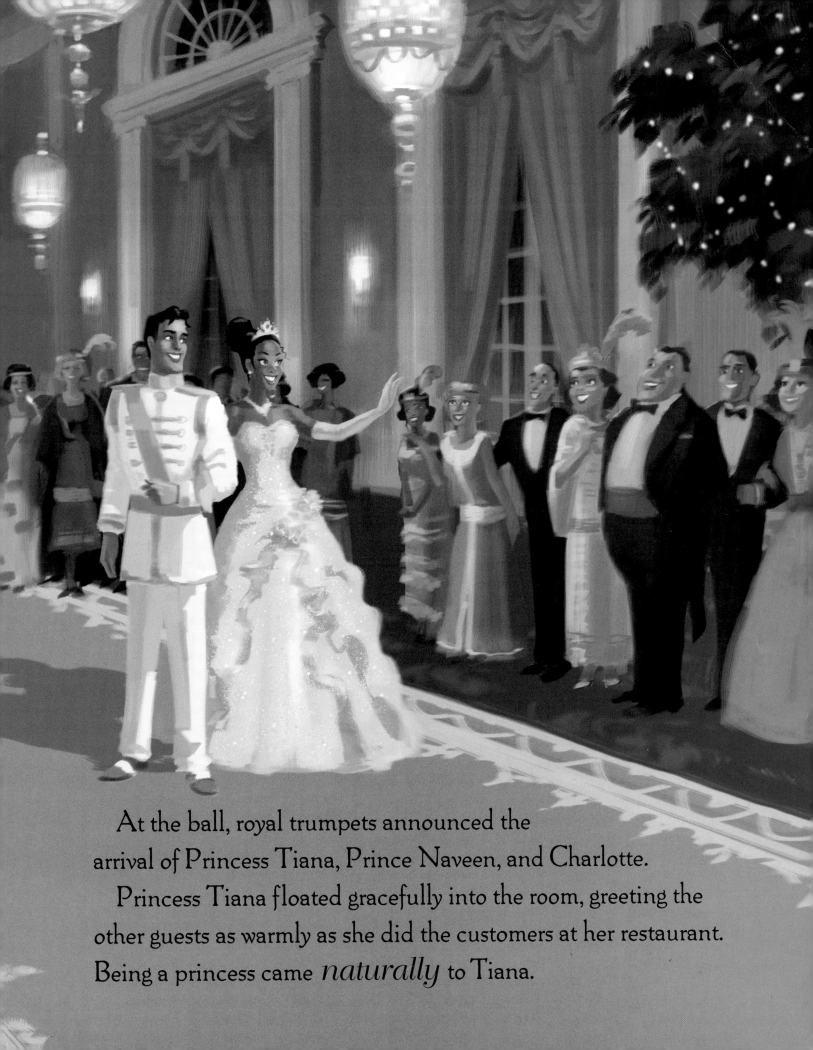

At the ball, royal trumpets announced the
arrival of Princess Tiana, Prince Naveen, and Charlotte.
Princess Tiana floated gracefully into the room, greeting the
other guests as warmly as she did the customers at her restaurant.
Being a princess came *naturally* to Tiana.

Charlotte tapped Tiana's shoulder. "There's just one more rule every princess should know: *have fun!*"

"Now, that's a rule to live by," Tiana said as she danced under the stars.